MADAME NIGHTINGALE
WILL SING TONIGHT

James Mayhew

A BANTAM LITTLE ROOSTER BOOK
NEW YORK · TORONTO · LONDON · SYDNEY · AUCKLAND

Also by James Mayhew

Katie's Picture Show

MADAME NIGHTINGALE WILL SING TONIGHT
A Bantam Little Rooster Book / June 1991

PRINTING HISTORY
Published in Great Britain by Orchard Books in 1990

Little Rooster is a trademark of Bantam Books, a division of Bantam Doubleday Dell
Publishing Group, Inc.

Library of Congress Cataloging-in-Publication Data

Mayhew, James
    Madame Nightingale will sing tonight/James Mayhew,
    p.   cm. "A Bantam little rooster book."
    Summary; The woodland animals' plans for staging an opera run afoul
when the prima donna develops stage fright. Includes basic information
about opera and a list of famous operas.
    ISBN 0-553-07100-9
    [1. Opera-Fiction.   2. Forest animals-Fiction.]   I. Title.
    PZ7.M4684 Mad 1990
    [E] – dc20   90-32893
                                                                        CIP
                                                                        AC

Published simultaneously in the United States and Canada

Bantam Books are published by Bantam Books, a division of Bantam Doubleday Dell
Publishing Group, Inc. Its trademark, consisting of the words "Bantam Books" and the
portrayal of a rooster, is Registered in U.S. Patent and Trademark Office and in other
countries. Marca Registrada. Bantam Books, 666 Fifth Avenue, New York, New York
10103.

PRINTED IN BELGIUM

0 9 8 7 6 5 4 3 2 1

One spring morning Squirrel woke up to find that
someone had left a big pile of rubbish at the bottom
of his tree.

"How nasty!" he said, as he hopped over the bits
and pieces looking for food. He was careful not to
get his tail dirty.

Badger came out of his sett to see what was going on.

"I'll never understand why people throw things away," said Squirrel. He never threw anything away.

Squirrel and Badger picked their way among the broken furniture, old carriages, torn clothes, tin cans, and soggy newspapers.

Just then they saw Rabbit. She was sitting inside an odd-shaped box, washing her ears.

"I think this must be a doll's house, don't you?" she said.

"No, no," said Badger. "It's a television. People look at them for hours on end, I'm told."

Squirrel didn't know what it was. But as he couldn't eat it, he wasn't very interested.

Owl came fluttering down
from the tree where he had
been trying to sleep.

"You woke me up," he said
crossly. "In any case, you're
all wrong. It's a toy theater
in which children put on plays."

"A theater! I've always wanted to act," said Rabbit. "Why don't we put on a play?"

"Or a ballet," said Badger.

Mouse popped up out of an old shoe. "How about an opera?" she said. She had, at one time, lived in a grand theater and had once seen an opera. She remembered thinking it was rather beautiful.

"Silly Mouse, who would sing in it?" said Squirrel. "You can't have an opera without singers."

"We could ask the Wood Warbler," said Mole, who had just poked his head out of his hole.

"Oh, no, you must have a star," said Mouse. "A prima donna!"

"Then why don't we ask Madame Nightingale?" said Owl. "She sings better than any other bird in the woods."

So they all rushed off to the
other side of the woods
to see Madame Nightingale.

Madame Nightingale was just finishing her spring cleaning.

"We've come to ask you to sing in our opera," said Squirrel.

"You'll be the star," said Mouse.

"Me? Sing in an opera? What a splendid idea," she said. "Which one do you have in mind?"

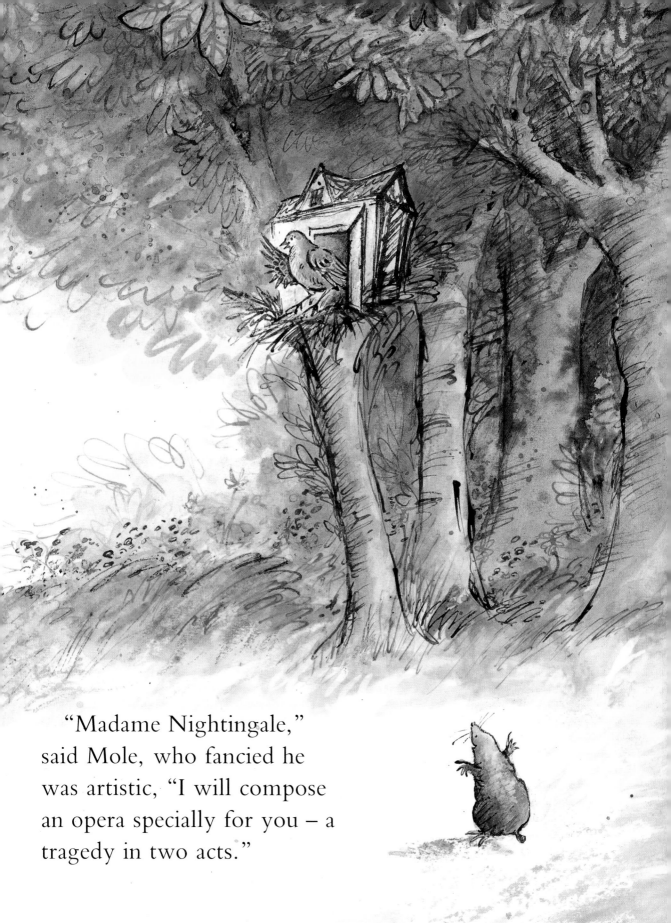

"Madame Nightingale,"
said Mole, who fancied he
was artistic, "I will compose
an opera specially for you – a
tragedy in two acts."

So they set to work in preparation of opening night.

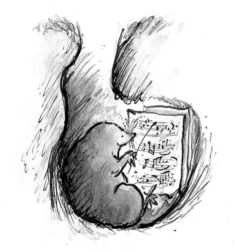

Mole was busy writing the music,

Mouse made the costumes,

Fox painted the scenery,

Rabbit sold the tickets,

and Squirrel and Badger put up the posters, while all
the other animals helped clear away the rubbish and
set up the toy theater.

On the day Mole finished his opera, he rushed to
Madame Nightingale's house to show it off.

"It looks marvelous, darling," said Madame
Nightingale. "Shall I try a bit?"

"Oh, yes!" said Mole, who felt terribly honored.
He sat down and waited. A great many small birds
gathered around to hear the great singer rehearse.

Madame Nightingale shut her eyes,
opened her beak,
filled her lungs,
and…

NOTHING CAME OUT!

What a commotion followed! Here was the prima donna, the star of the new opera, without a voice! Madame Nightingale nearly fainted from the shock.

Soon all the small birds had spread the news through the woods.

"Whatever shall we do?" said Badger. "Madame Nightingale has lost her voice, and Rabbit has already sold all the tickets."

"Where did she lose it?" asked Squirrel. "It must be somewhere."

"Don't be silly," said Badger. "We must find a cure for her. Fetch the doctor!"

Doctor Crow came at once. Madame Nightingale
drank potions, swallowed pills, and sucked lozenges,
but still her voice didn't come back.

Meanwhile, all the woodland animals lined up at Rabbit's ticket stall.

"I gave you four acorns for my ticket," said an angry hedgehog. "I want them back."

"And I want my berries back," said a thrush. "They were my nicest ones."

"We're trying to find a cure," shouted Rabbit. "You must be patient."

But the day before the opera was due to open, Madame Nightingale still hadn't gotten her voice back. That night Owl called all the woodland animals together.

"This desperate situation calls for drastic measures," said Owl. "Listen carefully everyone. I have a plan. . . ."

The next morning Badger and Squirrel put up posters announcing a change of cast: the Wood Warbler would star in the opera instead of Madame Nightingale.

It didn't take long for Madame Nightingale to discover that she had been replaced, and by her understudy at that.

Madame Nightingale had never been so angry in all her life. To think that her chance at stardom was being snatched away by a…Wood Warbler!

In a flurry of feathers, she flew straight to the clearing where there was a rehearsal going on.

"*What is the meaning of this outrage?*" she stormed.

There was a sudden silence in the woods.

"Your voice! It's come back!" Badger cried.

"You can sing for us after all," said Mole.

"Good gracious," said Madame Nightingale, with a quick trill or two. "But what about your new star, the Wood Warbler?"

"Well…" said Squirrel.

"Hmm…" said Badger.

"You see," said Owl, "You simply had a bad case of stage fright, and there is only one way around that. So with the help of the Wood Warbler we created a little off-stage drama of our own."

"I should be grateful, I suppose," said Madame Nightingale. "And I *shall* sing tonight after all."

So Squirrel and Badger changed the posters all over again to read:

Madame NIGHTINGALE Will Sing Tonight!

That night Madame Nightingale sang
better than she had ever sung before.

At the end of the opera, Mole, Badger, Rabbit,
Squirrel, Owl, Mouse, and all the animals clapped
and cheered until Madame Nightingale sang an
encore. The Wood Warbler was especially proud of
the role she had played. And in fact, no one could
remember ever having enjoyed himself so much!

Happily, Madame Nightingale never lost her voice again. And even when there isn't a new opera being staged, she can be heard singing on a summer evening, when all the other birds have gone to roost and the woods are silent.

More about Opera

Have you ever been to an opera? Perhaps you may have seen one on television. Or maybe you think opera is boring, something just for grown-ups. As all the animals in the story discovered, opera can be fun.

Opera is a play set to music. It tells a story through singing rather than speaking. Just as all the woodland animals had to work together on Madame Nightingale's opera, many people are needed to put together an opera for the stage.

A composer writes the music, a librettist writes the words to be sung, singers perform on stage in the theater, and an orchestra plays the music. And behind the scenes are an army of people who make the scenery and the costumes.

You can hear some opera music on the radio, on tape, or on a record. And if you have the chance to see an opera, either on television or in a theater, here are some of the many you might watch for and enjoy:

Die Zauberflöte (The Magic Flute)
Wolfgang Amadeus Mozart (1756-17

La Cenerentola (Cinderella)
Gioacchino Rossini (1792-1868)

Hänsel and Gretal
Engelbert Humperdinck (1854-1921)

Le Coq d'Or (The Golden Cockere
Nicolai Andreyevich Rimsky-
Korsakov (1844-1908)

The Little Sweep (from *Let's Make an Opera*) Benjamin Britten (1913-19

Amahl and the Night Visitors
Gian Carlo Menotti (born 1911)

Where the Wild Things Are
Oliver Knussen (born 1952)